SPORTS FUN

WRESTLING FUN

by Cari Meister

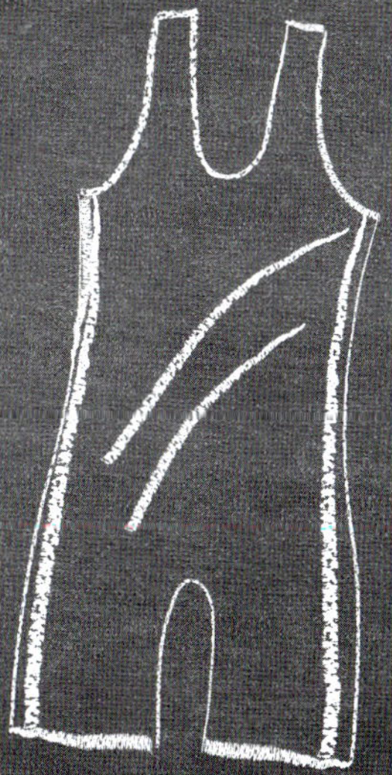

PEBBLE
a capstone imprint

Pebble Emerge is published by Pebble, an imprint of Capstone.
1710 Roe Crest Drive, North Mankato, Minnesota 56003
www.capstonepub.com

Library of Congress Cataloging-in-Publication Data
Names: Meister, Cari, author.
Title: Wrestling fun / by Cari Meister.
Description: North Mankato, Minnesota : Capstone Press, [2021] | Series: Sports fun | Includes bibliographical references and index. | Audience: Ages 6-8 | Audience: Grades 2-3 | Summary: "Wrestling is cool to watch, but it's even more fun to do! Kids can get out on the mat by learning the rules of the sport, the gear and skills needed to wrestle, and the importance of good sportsmanship. A skill-building activity helps readers get in on the fun"--Provided by publisher.
Identifiers: LCCN 2020037714 (print) | LCCN 2020037715 (ebook) | ISBN 9781977132307 (hardcover) | ISBN 9781977155405 (pdf) | ISBN 9781977157027 (kindle edition)
Subjects: LCSH: Wrestling--Juvenile literature.
Classification: LCC GV1195.3 .M45 2021 (print) | LCC GV1195.3 (ebook) | DDC 796.812--dc23
LC record available at https://lccn.loc.gov/2020037714
LC ebook record available at https://lccn.loc.gov/2020037715

Image Credits
Alamy: Jeramey Lende, 9, 11, 17; AP Photo: Amy Sancetta, 12, 19, Republican-Herald/Jacqueline Dormer, 15; Getty Images: Sergei Supinsky, 10; Newscom: ZUMA Press/News-Miner/Eric Engman, 13, 18; Shutterstock: A_Lesik, 16, Ahturner, cover, 5, 8, 14, 21, JoeSAPhotos, 7; SuperStock: age fotostock/Jim West, 6

Editorial Credits
Editor: Jill Kalz; Designer: Tracy McCabe; Media Researcher: Eric Gohl; Production Specialist: Katy LaVigne

All internet sites appearing in back matter were available and accurate when this book was sent to press.

Printed in the United States 4979

TABLE OF CONTENTS

Words in **bold** are in the glossary.

WHAT IS WRESTLING?

Two kids meet on a mat. They move around each other. Suddenly, one tries to **pin** the other. What are they doing? They are wrestling!

Wrestling is one of the oldest sports in the world. People have done it for more than 4,000 years.

There are three main kinds of wrestling: **folkstyle**, **freestyle**, and **Greco-Roman**. Each kind has different rules and moves. The goal is the same: Pin your **opponent**.

folkstyle wrestling

In folkstyle, people wrestle mostly down on the mat. In freestyle, they stand more and use their legs to trip and pin. Wrestlers in Greco-Roman cannot use their legs.

WHAT DO I NEED?

You need **headgear** to wrestle. It keeps your ears safe when they're hit. Special shoes keep your ankles from twisting. You may wear kneepads too.

Wrestlers wear a one-piece uniform called a singlet. It has no sleeves and short legs. It is stretchy and fits close to your body. It lets you move easily.

WHERE DO I WRESTLE?

Many schools have wrestling teams. Some fitness centers have special classes. There may be a sports club near you that you can join.

You wrestle in a large, open space. Gyms are good places. A thick mat covers the floor. It keeps you from getting hurt when you fall. It has two circles on it.

HOW DO I LEARN?

You learn to wrestle by doing drills. Drills are moves you do over and over. They help you learn how to move your arms, legs, and body the right way.

Your coach will break down each move into steps. You will practice the steps with a partner. To make it fair, your partner should weigh about the same as you.

Once you know the moves, you have contests called matches. You and your opponent start inside the small circle on the mat. You try to pin each other. You twist and flip. You grab and hold. You push and make your opponent lose their **balance**.

Funnel Cakes
French Fries

Sometimes, no one gets pinned. Who wins the match? Different moves get points. For example, you get a point if you break free from your opponent.

You also get points if the other wrestler doesn't follow the rules. If they're too rough or a bad sport, you get points. The person with the most points wins.

HOW CAN I BE A GOOD SPORT?

Being a good sport means playing fair and being kind. Follow the rules. Always listen to your coach.

Help your teammates if they need it. Be thankful for the help they give you. Win or lose, be nice. And have fun!

SKILL BUILDER: ON YOUR FEET

Balance is important in wrestling. Try this skill-building game to help you stay on your feet.

What You Need:

- a friend
- a soft floor mat

What You Do:

1. Stand barefoot on the mat, facing your friend.
2. Using your right hand, hold your right foot up behind you by the ankle. Have your friend do the same.
3. Start the game on the count of three. Use your free arms to try to push each other off-balance. The first person to drop their foot or fall down loses the round. The other person gets a point.

4. Play 10 rounds holding your right foot. Then switch to your left foot for another 10 rounds.

Tip: Use short hops when you get pushed. Hopping will help you keep your balance.

GLOSSARY

balance (BA-luhnts)—the state of being steady and not falling over

folkstyle (FOHK-stile)—a kind of wrestling that is done mostly down on the mat

freestyle (FREE-stile)—a kind of wrestling that is done mostly standing up and allows leg moves

Greco-Roman (GREH-koh-ROH-muhn)—a kind of wrestling that does not allow leg moves or grabs below the waist

headgear (HED-geer)—a covering for a wrestler's head with large cups to keep the ears safe

opponent (uh-POH-nuhnt)—the person who you are wrestling against

pin (PIN)—to bring a wrestler to the ground and hold their shoulders to the mat for two seconds

READ MORE

Fishman, Jon M. *Pro-Wrestling Superstar John Cena.* Minneapolis: Lerner Publications, 2019.

Rebman, Nick. *Wrestling.* Lake Elmo, MN: Focus Readers, 2019.

Sherman, Jill. *Wrestling.* Minneapolis: Bellwether Media, 2020.

INTERNET SITES

Olympic Wrestling Freestyle
https://www.olympic.org/wrestling-freestyle

Wrestling Facts for Kids
https://kids.kiddle.co/Wrestling

Wrestling Your Way to Fitness
https://www.kidzworld.com/article/6123-wrestling-your-way-to-fitness

INDEX